Rossi.

D-DAY

Henry Brook

Designed by Karen Tomlins

History consultant: Terry Charman, Imperial War Museums

Canadian soldiers fight their way out of the surf in Orville Fisher's, *The Assault*. Fisher was one of the few war artists who landed with the troops on D-Day.

Acknowledgements

© **Akg-images** *p58* Akg-images; © **Alamy** *Back cover* World War History, *p12* Kevin Howchin; © **The Bridgeman Art Library** *p1* Painting 'The Assualt' by Orville Fisher © Canadian War Museum, Ottawa, Canada, *p2-3* 'D Day', (oil on canvas), Cuneo, Terence (1907-96)/Private Collection, © Estate of Terence Cuneo/Bridgeman, *p4* 'The 1943 Quebec Conference' 1945, by Hubert Rogers. © Canadian War Museum, Ottawa, Canada, *p8-9* 'Dieppe Raid' (oil on canvas), Comfort, Charles Fraser (1900-1994)/© Canadian War Museum, Ottawa, Canada, *p18-19* H.M.S. 'Warspite' Engaging Enemy Batteries on D-Day Plus Two (oil on panel), Hamilton, John (1919-93)/© Army and Navy Club, London, UK/© Jane/Ed Hamilton, *p54-55* 'The Tanks Go In', Sword Beach (oil on canvas), Willis, Richard (Contemporary Artist) /Private Collection. © Richard Willis/Bridgeman, *p62t* Galerie Bilderwelt, *p64* Galerie Bilderwelt; © **Corbis** *Front cover* Hulton-Deutsch Collection, *p17* Hulton-Deutsch Collection, *p20t*, *p37* Bettmann, *p38* Ted Streshinsky, *p45*, *p52*, *p63* Bettmann; © **Getty Images** *p5* Hulton Archive, *p7* Gamma Keystone, *p13t* Keystone, *p13b* Keystone-France/Gamma-Keystone, *p20b* Roger Viollet, *p25* Office of Strategic Services/Interim Archives, *p26* Roger Viollet, *p29* Bob Landry//Time Life Pictures, *p30-31* Galerie Bilderwelt, *p35* Keystone, *p44* Galerie Bilderwelt, *p46* Time & Life Pictures, *p49b* Galerie Bilderwelt, *p56-57* Galerie Bilderwelt, *p60-61* Galerie Bilderwelt, *p61t* MPI; © **IWM** *p10* EA 33078, *p14-15b* EA 64465, *p16* MH 1997, *p21* HU 28594, *p23t* H 35179, *p23b* STT 9486, *p27* CL 1405, *p32* EA 25491, *p33* B 12153, *p34* H 39070, *p40* B5232, *p41* B5288, *p42-43b* A 23720A, *p48t* PL 25481, *p53* B 5245, *p57m* EA 25902, *p62b* 'Mulberry Harbour' by Stephen Bone, 1944 ART LD 5445; © **Magnum Photos** *p50-51* © Robert Capa © International Center of Photography; © **Mary Evans Picture Library** *p39* Illustrated London News Ltd, *p47* Robert Hunt Library; © **PA Photos** *p48br* AP/Press Association Images; © **Topfoto** *22* 2004 Topham Picturepoint; **U.S. National Archives** *p42t* Army Signal Corps Collection, *p59* US Army Collections.

Many of the photographs in this book were originally in black and white and have been digitally tinted by Usborne Publishing.

Usborne Quicklinks

You can find out more about D-Day by going to the Usborne Quicklinks Website at www.usborne-quicklinks.com and typing in the keywords 'yr d-day'.
Please note Usborne Publishing cannot be responsible for the content of any website other than its own.

Contents

This painting of D-Day, by British artist Terence Cuneo, shows the frenzy of battle on June 6, 1944.

The countries at war with Hitler were known as the Allies. This painting by Hubert Rogers shows a 1943 conference between Allied leaders in Quebec, Canada.

CHAPTER 1
Fortress Europe

In the summer of 1943, British and American commanders faced one of the toughest decisions of the Second World War. They were gathering troops and weapons to launch a crushing attack against the German forces occupying Western Europe.

But where was the best place to open battle and go on to win the War?

Over three years of horror, bloodshed and chaos had followed the start of combat in September 1939, after the German army, the mighty *Wehrmacht*, crashed into Poland. The governments of France and Britain had sworn to protect Poland and they quickly declared war on Germany.

Hitler's elite soldiers had conquered Poland, France and much of Europe, before invading the Soviet Union in 1941. A Japanese attack on the American naval base at Pearl Harbor brought the United States into the conflict later the same year.

The German leader, Adolf Hitler, salutes a company of his infantry marching into Poland. As the war spread, Japan and Italy joined forces with Hitler in a group called the Axis Powers.

After a run of dazzling and rapid triumphs in their early campaigns, *Wehrmacht* forces were stretched too thin, too far and they began to suffer defeats. By 1943, German troops had been defeated in the deserts of North Africa, they were under siege in Italy, and fighting for their lives deep inside the Soviet Union.

Soviet units faced the bulk of the *Wehrmacht* war machine alone and Stalin urged Churchill and Roosevelt to do more.

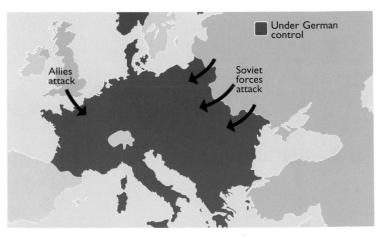

This map shows how an invasion in the West would trap the German army between Soviet and Allied forces.

If British and US soldiers landed in France, the Germans would have to split their army between two battlefronts. With the enemy divided and weakened, the Allies could then press towards Berlin, the capital city and heart of Germany.

But the Allies had a problem. Although the *Wehrmacht* was battered, it was by no means beaten. The Germans had occupied areas of France and Belgium bordering the English Channel, and had studded every cliff and beach with concrete bunkers, minefields and massive guns. Hitler called this his Atlantic Wall and boasted that it made Europe an impregnable fortress.

Massive German guns guarded the sea routes to France.

Early raids along the coast had ended in disaster. In August 1942, 6,000 Canadian, British and US troops stormed the port of Dieppe. Outgunned by German defenders, most of the attackers were trapped on the beach. More than half the Allied soldiers were killed, wounded or captured before British Royal Navy ships could rescue them.

Despite this, the Allies had little choice but to plan a fresh assault on the Atlantic Wall. Nobody expected Hitler to stop fighting until his ground forces had been decimated and his capital had fallen. Even in 1941, Winston Churchill had told

Canadian war artist Charles Comfort shows commandos storming the beach in his painting, *Dieppe Raid*.

his generals: "Unless we can go and land and fight Hitler and beat his forces on land, we shall never win this war."

Allied commanders understood their strike into Europe would be an extraordinary gamble, with thousands of lives and future victory in the War at stake. The military codename for the date of the attack was *D-Day* – and the name stuck. It's used by millions of people today to describe the largest and most daring seaborne invasion the world has ever seen.

CHAPTER 2
A winning plan

T he man with the task of proposing where, when and how to smash through the Atlantic Wall was British Lieutenant General Frederick Morgan. He used the initials of his job as Chief of Staff to the Supreme Allied Commander to name his planning team: COSSAC. The Allies needed a codename for their mission to reconquer Europe and Churchill selected the rather grand title: *Overlord*.

By April 1943, COSSAC had recruited experts from across the Allied forces. They quickly decided on France as the best site to land an army, with two possible locations: Pas de Calais or Normandy.

General Morgan, one of the chief planners of *Operation Overlord*, at his desk

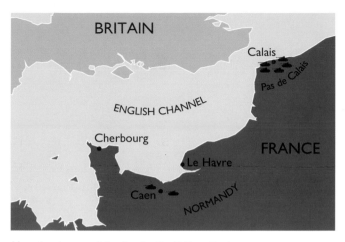

Map showing possible sites for the D-Day attack

There were good reasons for choosing northern France. The region was dotted with sandy beaches, ideal for landing troops from the sea, and it was close to Britain. The southern counties could serve as the base for assembling stores, weapons and men to build a powerful army.

COSSAC believed that three infantry divisions, each with around 20,000 soldiers, would be needed for D-Day. They could approach France in an armada of Allied warships, before charging onto the beaches from small landing craft.

This part of the invasion took the codename, *Neptune*, and it was decided that the earliest possible date for the attack would be May 1, 1944.

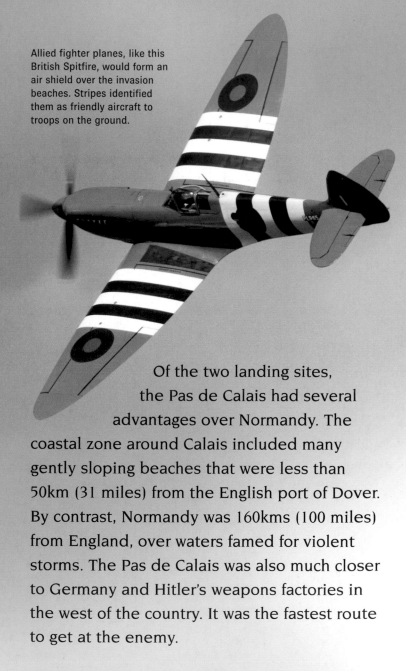

Allied fighter planes, like this British Spitfire, would form an air shield over the invasion beaches. Stripes identified them as friendly aircraft to troops on the ground.

Of the two landing sites, the Pas de Calais had several advantages over Normandy. The coastal zone around Calais included many gently sloping beaches that were less than 50km (31 miles) from the English port of Dover. By contrast, Normandy was 160kms (100 miles) from England, over waters famed for violent storms. The Pas de Calais was also much closer to Germany and Hitler's weapons factories in the west of the country. It was the fastest route to get at the enemy.

German defenders were dug in along the coast.

The Pas de Calais was a tantalizing prize. But the Germans knew this only too well and had made it their chief stronghold on the Atlantic Wall, guarded by elite troops, fighter planes and some of their best *Panzer* tank divisions. COSSAC decided it was too tough a nut to crack and so turned their gaze towards Normandy.

The commander of this German heavy tank, known as a *Panzer*, is using binoculars to scout the battlefield.

At first glance, the Normandy coast looked wild and edged with cliffs, but COSSAC planners noticed a chain of five, sandy beaches between the ports of Le Havre and Cherbourg. Both towns had huge guns covering their sea approaches, leaving the beaches less well defended. The Germans were not expecting an attack here. It was too far from England and there was no sheltered mooring place for ships to offload supplies for an invading army.

Putting distance and anchorage problems aside, the Allies picked Normandy as the location for the D-Day landings.

The Germans had fixed a maze of posts into the sands, topping them with mines that exploded on contact with passing boats.

COSSAC then began one of the most complex and in-depth spying missions ever attempted. They needed to learn the secrets of the beaches – including tests on whether the sand and soil was firm enough to bear the weight of a tank.

Throughout the winter of 1943, Allied planes photographed every inch of the Normandy coast. Commando units made secret night raids, to collect explosive mines and obstacles from the shallows. Each device was dismantled and tested so that engineers would know how to make them safe. The British even sent midget submarines to spy on the beaches. On the eve of D-Day, the crew of one sub watched German soldiers playing football across the dunes.

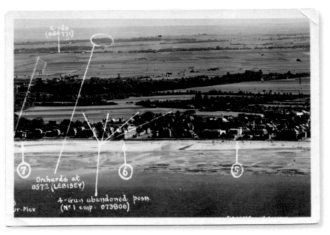

Coastal details marked on a travel photograph

COSSAC left no stone unturned. Earlier in the War, the BBC had appealed to its radio listeners to send in any postcards, brochures and photographs from their European travels.

As a result, the British government had received millions of these images. COSSAC agents began sifting through the collection, checking the position of every hill, house and landmark against aerial spy pictures.

The Allies were certain that their intense preparations would reduce the risk of bloodshed for the attacking soldiers. But nobody expected the landings to be easy: there were a million things that could go fatally wrong.

CHAPTER 3

Taking command

In January 1944, COSSAC handed responsibility for *Overlord* to the US general picked by Roosevelt as Supreme Commander of the Allied invasion. Dwight 'Ike' Eisenhower was an experienced commander who had already overseen amphibious invasions against the Axis in North Africa and Sicily. He was a talented organizer who understood the needs of his soldiers and made key changes to improve the battle plan.

General Eisenhower
in a US Jeep

Eisenhower and his staff had agreed that the first wave of troops should land at dawn, to surprise the defenders. In the hours before D-Day, thousands of Allied bombers would fly missions along the coast, smashing any concrete fortifications. Floating barges armed with rockets, and warships from the invasion fleet, would join the thunderous barrage of fire directed at the shoreline while the landing craft approached.

The planners hoped any surviving defenders would be too stunned by the noise and smoke to put up much of a fight. *Overlord* was a massive operation. While Eisenhower remained in overall charge, he picked a British general, Bernard Montgomery, to command all ground units.

This battle painting by British army officer John Hamilton is entitled *H.M.S. Warspite Engaging Enemy Batteries on D-Day Plus Two.*

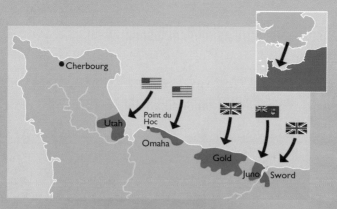

Naming the beaches

'Monty', as he was known to his troops, was an aggressive and straight-talking leader who had helped to defeat the Germans in North Africa. He insisted on doubling the D-Day infantry force to at least six divisions: more than 120,000 men. Each landing beach was given its own codename and attack force. The Americans would capture *Omaha* and *Utah*. *Gold* and *Sword* were British targets and the Canadians had to take *Juno*.

Montgomery knew that winning the beaches would be a bloody struggle. He had first-hand experience of battling the new commander of the Atlantic Wall, Field Marshal Erwin Rommel.

General Bernard L. Montgomery watches his tanks advance toward German lines. North Africa, November 1942.

Rommel (right) earned his nickname, 'the Desert Fox', fighting alongside Italian allies. Here, he studies the order of battle with an Italian general.

A star among Hitler's *Wehrmacht* elite, Rommel was a cunning and daring general who had clashed with Montgomery across Egypt and Libya. Hitler had asked his Desert Fox to shore up the Atlantic Wall around the time that Eisenhower arrived in London.

On an inspection tour of northern France, Rommel was shocked by how inadequately the beaches were defended. He ordered a massive construction project to bolster the Wall, making his troops lay minefields, pour concrete for bunkers and cover the beaches in obstacles that would rip holes in approaching ships. The Atlantic Wall in Normandy was getting a lot tougher.

Rommel inspecting his Atlantic Wall defences

The Allies turned to their scientists and engineers for help clearing Rommel's beach obstacles. Teams of combat engineers volunteered to join the first wave of attack boats, disarming German mines and explosive traps to open safe channels into the landing areas.

Special swimming tanks were designed to reach the beaches just ahead of the troops, with the firepower to blast holes in barbed wire and concrete barriers. Boxed with canvas screens, the tanks displaced just enough water to stay afloat in gentle seas. They could be launched from Landing Craft Tank ships close to shore and had propellers turned by their own engines.

The Germans welded steel girders together to make these beach obstacles, which were known as 'hedgehogs'.

British tank crews prepare for a trial run in their swimming tanks.

British engineers adapted other tanks to clear minefields with spinning chains or carry huge bundles of wood to fill ditches. Soldiers nicknamed these odd-looking machines 'the Funnies'. Hundreds of them went into action on D-Day across the British and Canadian beaches.

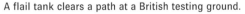

A flail tank clears a path at a British testing ground.

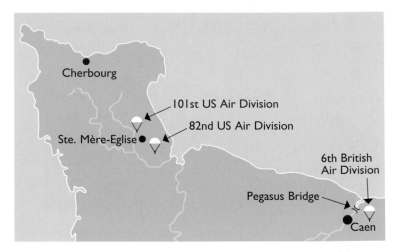

More than ten thousand paratroopers formed an advance guard around the beach landings.

Like many in the German High Command, Rommel was convinced that Eisenhower would land his army at the Pas de Calais. But he didn't agree with Hitler's order to keep most of the *Panzer* divisions away from the coast, ready to fight in rolling, open country. Rommel believed the only way to beat the invasion was to kill it dead on the beaches. The moment any Allied units landed, he wanted to pin them on the sand before rushing soldiers and tanks forward to encircle and destroy the attack.

Eisenhower and Montgomery thought they could use airborne troops to stay one step ahead of the Desert Fox. Only hours before the landings, thousands of Allied soldiers would strike deep inland, carried by gliders or dropped by parachute. These paratroopers had orders to capture bridges, roads and other transport links, before the Germans could bring up support troops and weapons.

Paratroopers were also given the task of protecting the open sides, or flanks, of the invasion forces. British 6th Airborne Division would guard the east and knock out enemy gun installations, while two divisions of US paratroopers, the 101st and 82nd Airborne, dropped to the west to seize all roads leading to Cherbourg and the *Omaha* and *Utah* beaches.

A strong German garrison protected the port of Cherbourg. Like many towns in Normandy, it was badly damaged by Allied bombing raids.

The Allies had other tactics and tricks to wrong-foot Rommel. They realized that the Germans would notice the huge build-up of troops, ships and equipment around English ports in advance of D-Day, but they found ways to use all this activity to their advantage.

If the Germans could be persuaded that the invasion was really directed at the Pas de Calais, it would tie up thousands of enemy soldiers and heavy weapons. And so the Allies began a game of deception and double-dealing.

Troops lift a rubber decoy
tank into position.

A British bomber drops a cargo of foil strips, known as 'chaff'.

In *Operation Bodyguard*, Allied intelligence agents used an array of decoy tactics to distract the German army from the real target.

A 'ghost army' of radio operators moved to a base in Scotland, sending enough messages over the airwaves to convince German eavesdroppers that a large battle group was planning to attack in Norway. Another ghost army appeared in Kent, poised to strike at targets above France.

On D-Day itself, the Allies fooled German RADAR technicians by dropping millions of tiny metal strips from RAF planes. RADAR signals bounce off metal and the Germans mistook the strips for a great fleet of planes and ships rushing at Calais.

Perhaps the most persuasive warnings about a Pas de Calais raid came from the enemy's own snoopers. British security groups intercepted German spies trying to enter England secretly and offered them a brutal choice. They could face prison and possible execution for espionage, or help the Allies.

In the months before D-Day, the German agents sent a steady stream of radio messages to their spymasters, all reporting a build-up of troops and weapons for an attack on the Pas de Calais.

The British also recruited agents who pretended to support the Axis nations. One Allied spy, codename *Garbo*, even won a medal from Adolf Hitler, in reward for his intelligence reports – all fake.

In the spring of 1944, military camps, tanks and weapons stores began to appear around the villages and towns of southern England. Tucked away from German spotter planes, the huge Allied army was waiting for the right weather and tides for their assault on Normandy. D-Day had already been postponed until the first week of June. Now, a fleet of 6,000 ships stood ready to carry the army into battle. After a year of feverish planning and preparation, battle was coming to the quiet beaches of France.

Allied weapons, vehicles and stores stand ready for the invasion.

CHAPTER 4
Night raiders

The Allies had tested and checked every detail of the *Overlord* plan, but they couldn't control the weather. Eisenhower asked meteorologists to predict the best dates in May and June for calm seas and low tides. Ideally, he also wanted cloudless skies before dawn to help his paratroopers reach their targets safely. Weather expert James Stagg thought June 5 would be clear and calm across Normandy. Eisenhower ordered the invasion fleet to be ready to sail for France on the night of June 4.

In the first days of June, the Allied army stirred into life. All along England's southern coast, from Falmouth to Portsmouth, roads teemed with soldiers and vehicles making their way to quayside loading areas. By June 3, the invasion fleet was waiting outside the ports, fully loaded with men and machines for the Channel crossing.

But, on the morning of June 4, Stagg hit Eisenhower with a bombshell: "A storm's blowing in," Stagg announced. "The sea will be too rough for the landing ships to get to shore."

Loading troops and supplies onto the battle fleet at a port at a secret location on England's southern coast

Eisenhower knew that off-loading the troops would cause days of disruption and delays. So he ordered the fleet to wait at anchor, hoping for a break in the storm. While soldiers battled boredom and seasickness on the rocking boats, Stagg made new calculations. He returned to Allied Headquarters that same evening, to inform Eisenhower there was a good chance the storm would clear by June 6. Eisenhower took a gamble and gave the order to go.

General Eisenhower talks to the men who will risk their lives on D-Day.

Special Forces paratroopers were among the first troops to go into battle on D-Day. These 'pathfinders' flew into the dark in the opening minutes of June 6, with orders to plant radio beacons at strategic points across Normandy. The three airborne divisions of more than 20,000 men could then follow the beacon signals to their landing zones.

At airbases across England, waiting paratroopers crammed into transport planes. Each man carried almost his own bodyweight in food rations, weapons and ammunition. He had to be ready to fight the instant he hit the ground.

The portable, PIAT - Projector Infantry Anti-Tank - hurled an explosive charge that could knock out tanks and heavy vehicles.

British Pathfinder officers check their watches in the last minutes of June 5, 1944. They would soon be leaping into dark skies above France.

Not long after midnight, waves of transport planes crossed the French coast, coming under heavy fire from German ground forces. Stagg's predictions for the storm's passing had been correct, but there were patches of bad weather still lurking above Normandy. With shells exploding around them, many of the paratroopers had to jump into banks of cloud, with no clear view of the terrain below.

It took less than a minute for them to reach the ground. They landed in woods, marshes and other rough country, peering into the gloom as

This picture of an Allied airdrop over southern France shows how easily troops could drift off their target.

the earth rushed towards them. Most of the soldiers found that they had drifted far from their targets - and from each other. They were lost in enemy territory and had to waste hours trying to regroup.

Allied gliders soon appeared in the skies above the confusion, bringing more troops and heavier weapons to the drop zones. But there were trees, hedgerows and other obstacles dotted about the fields and many of the gliders crashed on landing, killing the soldiers and crew inside. D-Day was only a few hours old but already the air assault seemed to be failing.

The paratroopers were aided by the work of a secret army fighting inside France: the Resistance, or *Maquis*. These local people were experts in sabotage missions, destroying or interrupting German army transport links and communications. Resistance members had cut telephone wires across Normandy, making it difficult for German commanders to contact their posts and discover the real size and location of the Allied paratrooper attack.

Resistance fighters also wrecked railway tracks and trains, blocking German reinforcements from reaching the coast.

An American officer swaps intelligence with French resistance fighters.

They passed information on the Atlantic Wall to the Allies by secret radio messages. On the night before D-Day, the BBC had included some codewords in a news broadcast that could be picked up in France. The phrase, "the dice are on the carpet," meant that the day of invasion – and liberation from the German occupiers – was finally coming.

Soldiers from 82nd Airborne Division had been tasked with capturing Ste. Mère-Eglise, a small town between Cherbourg and the American beaches. Dozens accidentally drifted onto the town while German troops were trying to extinguish a house fire. They were revealed by light from the blaze and the Germans shot many of them before they could struggle out of their parachute straps.

One unfortunate paratrooper, John Steele, snagged his parachute on the steeple of the town's church. He was trapped, hanging by a thread, until the Germans took him prisoner. Steele later escaped and found his way back to friends.

Though dazed and disorientated after their scattered landings, the US paratroopers managed to regroup into a fighting force. A few hours later,

A dummy of John Steele hangs from the church tower at Ste. Mère-Eglise to mark the anniversary of D-Day.

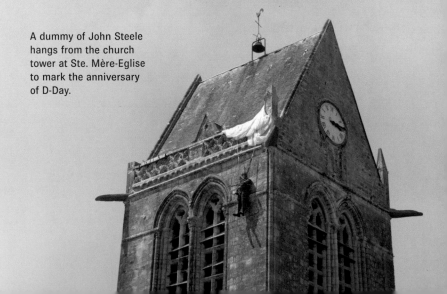

around 200 paratroopers
stormed and captured
the town from the
Germans. Next, they
set up roadblocks and
searched the woods
for stragglers, growing
stronger in numbers as
the sun began to rise.

A moment's rest after a
hard-won battle

While the Americans
battled in the west,
British airborne soldiers
were landing to the east
and fighting hard. One of their boldest attacks was
at a canal crossing now known as Pegasus Bridge.
This was a difficult and high-risk mission, not least
because the paratroopers had orders to capture
two bridges intact.

The crossing was close to the town of Caen,
only a few miles from the British and Canadian
beaches. Montgomery wanted to stop the
Germans tanks from getting over the canal to fight
the invasion, but the crossing might also be useful
for Allied vehicles in the coming hours. Monty
believed his commandos had a good chance of

snatching Caen before the close of D-Day. Major John Howard was ordered to seize the bridges, aided by British 6th Airborne.

Howard and his assault team of around 180 airborne infantrymen were the first British soldiers to land in France on D-Day. They arrived silently in six gliders, slewing across a grassy field and halting only a few hundred feet from their target.

The guards at the crossing were terrified by the sight of enemy soldiers charging out of the night. After a quick firefight, the British forced them off the canal and set up machine-gun posts overlooking the roads to the bridges.

Glider landings were dangerous, but they delivered troops into the thick of the action.

It was a long night for the Major and his men, battling all attempts by the enemy to recapture the bridge. But they were reinforced by passing British paratroopers and commandos and they held fast, well into D-Day.

Howard knew that help was on its way. Out at sea, a fleet of ships carried an army of Allied soldiers towards the beaches. The land invasion was about to begin.

Pegasus Bridge with one of the crashed gliders in the background

American troops march through an English port to board their transport ships.

CHAPTER 5
To the beaches

British minesweepers set off first, clearing a safe route across the English Channel for the Allied armada. Six thousand warships, troop transports, hospital ships and landing craft loaded with tanks followed their course through the evening of June 5. Anything that could float had been ordered into the fleet. It was an all-or-nothing invasion.

The Allied leaders understood that if D-Day failed it would set their war effort back a year or more. But the men playing cards, trying to rest or write letters between the rolling decks of the fleet had more immediate concerns – staying alive in the next few hours. Eisenhower summed up the mood of many in his speech to the departing army.

"Your task will not be an easy one. Your enemy is well-trained, well-equipped and battle hardened. He will fight savagely.

But this is the year 1944! Much has happened... the tide has turned! The free men of the world are marching together to victory! I have full confidence in your courage... we will accept nothing less than full victory! Good luck."

This picture shows hundreds of ships from the invasion fleet massing off the Isle of Wight, southern England.

American soldiers board a transport ship bound for *Omaha* Beach.

Most of the men on the big troop transports were too excited to sleep. They joined the breakfast lines in the small hours and ate platefuls of hot food to sustain them though the coming battle. But, after climbing down rope nets to the small, bobbing craft that would carry them to shore, many of the soldiers began to feel queasy. The sea was still lively after the storm and within a few minutes the landing boats were reeking with puddles of sick. Packed tightly together, some of the men had no choice but to empty their stomachs into their helmets.

The landing craft wheeled and bucked as they formed up into attack waves. It was too dangerous to take the massive warships and troop transports any closer to shore, where they would be within range of enemy guns.

Sweating, seasick and soaked to the skin, each man in the boats carried almost 30kg (70lbs) of weapons and equipment. Staring up at the sky they watched hundreds of high, black crosses moving steadily towards France. The Allied bombers were on their way to blast the coast with explosive shells.

Soldiers climb down to a beach landing craft, also known as a Higgins boat after its inventor.

The hulls of the landing craft were built high to protect the soldiers from bomb-splinter shrapnel and machine-gun bullets. But any man peering over the side would have seen a line of fire crackling along the horizon. Many Allied bomber crews flew two missions on D-Day, gouging craters from the beaches and cliffs to clear the way for the troops.

An Allied Marauder bomber with friendly markings

It was still dark when the first wave of landing ships began their 5km (3 miles) journey to shore. The men were scheduled to reach the sands at dawn, close to 06:30. On their way to the beaches they had to cover their ears, as the big guns on the warships started to roar.

Six mighty battleships opened fire, joined by dozens of destroyers, the floating rocket barges and smaller fighting ships. The biggest shells were the size of a man and powerful enough to lift whole *Panzers* into the air. Soldiers watched in awe as they motored forwards over the sea.

When they were still 2kms (1 mile) from the beach, some of the men noticed large waterspouts bursting up from the waves. Not all the German guns had been knocked out by the air strikes or the warship barrage. The landing ships were coming under fire and the seasick raiders may have wondered if this was part of the *Overlord* plan.

A rocket barge from the Allied fleet opens fire.

Landing craft came in many sizes. These are landing craft tank ships to carry troops and heavy vehicles.

Not everything was going well for the swimming tanks, due to arrive on the beaches just minutes before the infantry. Crews had been shocked by the rough seas on the crossing to France. Their machines only had low, canvas screens to keep the water out and some crews had to launch more than 3kms (2 miles) from the shore.

This landing craft infantry ship is damaged and trying to offload troops.

Each landing craft carried four or five Sherman tanks. Many crews rolled down the ramps into a pitching sea only to tilt wildly on the waves. These unlucky tanks capsized and sank quickly, some taking their trapped crews with them.

In most cases, the closer the crews came to shore before unloading, the better chance their tanks had of floating. And hundreds of Shermans and other adapted tanks did survive the crossing, helping to support troops as they fought their way up the beaches.

Higgins boats had flat-bottomed hulls to slide over sand and a drop-down front ramp. They carried a platoon of around 30 fighting men.

When the first wave of infantry soldiers was close enough to land to see houses and other landmarks, some heard bullets thudding into the steel plates protecting the hulls of their boats. Machine gunners on the high ground above the beaches had opened fire. As the landing craft nudged past any hedgehogs or debris floating in the shallows, the men braced themselves for action.

The second the front ramp crashed down, they had to charge forwards into the surf. Many soldiers discovered their ships had caught on sandbars, so they had to wade or swim to the beach. Most arrived soaking wet, exhausted and seasick, but relieved to be on dry land, at last. Now they could get on with the fight.

The German heavy guns on the sheer cliffs at Pointe du Hoc were a threat to the Allied fleet. Ten landing ships of elite US Rangers had to scale the 30m (100 feet) cliffs and knock out the guns. They used rocket-propelled grappling hooks and ladders borrowed from the London Fire Brigade to reach the top, battling snipers and grenade-throwing defenders every step of the way.

The Rangers cut through a tangle of barbed wire at the cliff edge and captured the installation – but the guns were missing. Later on D-Day, Ranger scouts tracked them down and destroyed them. The heroism of the US Rangers is remembered today by a stark granite memorial surrounded by old bomb craters atop the Point du Hoc cliffs.

This image of soldiers charging onto *Omaha* Beach was taken by famous war photographer Robert Capa. Although the film was damaged, it captures the mood and chaos of the landings.

Helping the wounded up the beach

CHAPTER 6
D-Day heroes

Each of the five beaches had its different challenges and dangers, but they all had to be won. A single man in a machine-gun pillbox could do terrible damage among the ranks of soldiers slowly wading out of the sea. And there were thousands of these defenders along the coast, hiding in underground tunnels and behind minefields, launching explosive mortar shells over the heads of the attackers.

As one Allied survivor of D-Day put it, arriving on the beaches was, "like a visit into hell".

The huge Allied shells in the early bombardment had been effective along the British beaches. At *Gold*, as the first wave of landing craft arrived with the low tide at 07:30, British soldiers saw houses in flames and bomb craters scooped from the dunes.

There were no steep hills or cliffs to scale and the British quickly overran the dazed defenders, taking many prisoners. But Montgomery's troops still had to fight hard. They were shelled all through D-Day by German artillery and mortars.

Gold was the scene of a startling act of bravery, when Sergeant Major Stanley Hollis stormed two pillboxes to capture more than 20 men.

British commandos make their landing on *Gold* Beach.

His daring earned him the Victoria Cross medal, the highest recognition of bravery in the British military. Hollis was the only man to receive one out of 70,000 British troops who landed on D-Day.

Around 30,000 British soldiers made their landing at *Sword*. This beach ran straight onto a small town and there were German machine guns and artillery hidden among the houses.

The first waves of Higgins boats overtook their swimming tanks while still out at sea. Arriving first, the soldiers had little cover from enemy fire and hundreds were injured or killed.

This painting, *The Tanks Go In*, by Richard Willis, shows British tanks clearing barbed wire and hedgehogs on *Sword* Beach.

As the tanks reached the shore, the defenders gasped at the sight of giant, black machines rising out of the sea. Flail tanks quickly cleared a beach minefield and the British infantry rushed through the gap and into the town. They were soon fighting their way inland towards Caen.

Like the British beaches, *Juno* was overlooked by town houses and gun emplacements. But the Allied shelling hadn't managed to break the concrete walls of the biggest German forts. The Canadian soldiers also had to tackle a high sea wall at the top of the beach that prevented vehicles from leaving the sand.

The first Canadians landed at 08:00 and fought one of the toughest actions of D-Day. Under fire from machine guns and mortars, the force of around 20,000 men suffered over one thousand casualties before nightfall.

Every man in the Canadian assault was a volunteer and they were determined to have their revenge for the bloody failure at Dieppe. Sending tanks and bulldozers forward to demolish the sea wall, they took control of the beach and pressed on, into the town.

Meanwhile, at *Utah*, US combat engineers also used bulldozers to breach a sea wall. Soldiers sheltered behind slow-moving swimming tanks, taking cover from machine-gun fire. They followed the tanks through the sea wall gap before overwhelming the defenders.

Soldiers carry their equipment off the beach. Notice the men wheeling bicycles.

The first wave of 600 men came ashore at the wrong end of *Utah*, after currents pushed their boats off-course. But their officers managed to regroup and lead the force into the dunes, in some cases surprising the defenders with flank attacks.

Utah's battle group was a similar size to the Canadian force at *Juno*, but the Americans lost fewer than 200 soldiers.

Scaling the sea wall on *Utah* Beach

For the Allies, *Omaha* was the unluckiest, and the bloodiest, of all the beaches. Few of the swimming tanks survived the rough crossing. Their absence left the first waves of soldiers exposed to machine gun and rifle bullets, and the defenders had commanding views from their pillboxes in the steep hills or bluffs that overlooked every inch of the beach.

Part of *Omaha* was covered in a wall of loose pebbles, which blocked the way for heavy vehicles. The Germans also had long-range field guns that could knock out the approaching landing craft. Hundreds of soldiers had to leap into deep water from burning ships. Almost half the men in the first assault wave were cut down by murderous fire from the bluffs.

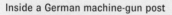
Inside a German machine-gun post

When they dragged themselves out of the surf, there was nowhere for the raiders to hide from the gunners dug-in above them. In all the smoke and confusion of battle, they looked for leaders to help guide them up the beach and into the attack. But many of the *Omaha* officers had died trying to get to the shore. Hundreds of men crawled or staggered to the shingle and took shelter as best as they could.

In the first hours at *Omaha*, many of the soldiers must have thought they would never get off the beach alive.

US navy officer Dwight Shepler shows the carnage and destruction on *Omaha* in his painting, *The Tough Beach*.

Wars are huge, world-changing events that affect millions of people. But winning a battle is down to the actions of individual soldiers and whether they are willing to risk their lives helping their friends and fighting for what they believe to be true and right. So it was on *Omaha*.

Slowly, small groups of men picked themselves up and started making their way forwards into the bluffs. The surviving officers gathered any soldiers who could walk and fight into platoons, leading them through the minefields and nests of barbed wire. Engineers started clearing safe paths and all the time fresh troops and weapons were arriving on shore.

Mission accomplished on *Omaha* Beach

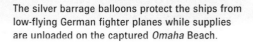

The silver barrage balloons protect the ships from
low-flying German fighter planes while supplies
are unloaded on the captured *Omaha* Beach.

A group of German prisoners waits gloomily behind rolls of barbed wire.

As the day wore on, the Americans climbed steadily through the hills, fighting skirmishes and taking prisoners as they captured the vital roadways that led to the beaches. Before nightfall, 30,000 troops had landed on *Omaha*. Over 2,000 had been wounded or killed during the battle – but the beach was won.

After a long day of savage combat, five beaches and 80kms (50 miles) of the Normandy coast were in Allied hands.

Within days of the landings, the Allies had built an artificial docking port, called a Mulberry, made up of floating barges and platforms. The white cross in the foreground of this painting by British artist Stephen Bone reminds us of the sacrifices made on D-Day.

CHAPTER 7
Victory earned

More than 150,000 troops landed in enemy-occupied Normandy on D-Day. They fought in a patchwork army of united nations, all with the single aim of defeating Hitler and the Axis Powers. Most of these soldiers had been civilians only a year or two earlier, with no experience of bloody warfare. Their attack on Normandy was a stunning achievement.

Up to 10,000 Allied troops had been killed or injured. But, given the risks of their mission, that number was almost miraculously low. Their leaders had expected far more men to die.

Two giants from the British war effort, Winston Churchill and General Montgomery, pay their respects to soldiers who fought on D-Day.

At the close of D-Day, Caen was still in German hands. But Eisenhower's forces had arrived and, despite desperate efforts by Hitler's best soldiers, they could not be halted.

As night fell on June 6, 1944, the exhausted invaders tried to heat some food and find a dry place to sleep. The Allies had taken the first step towards liberating Western Europe and won a victory that would help end the Second World War.

French civilians gave Allied soldiers a hero's welcome.

Edited by Jane Chisholm
Photographic manipulation by Keith Furnival and John Russell
Picture research: Ruth King

First published in 2014 by Usborne Publishing Ltd., Usborne House, 83-85 Saffron Hill, London EC1N 8RT, England. www.usborne.com
Copyright © 2014 Usborne Publishing Ltd.